ANTONIO EXPLORES SPACE

written and illustrated
by Rachel White

For my little newphew Antonio,
celebrating his first trip around the sun
and all the exploring that is yet to come!

Antonio prepared for a big adventure,
to go all the way to outer space!

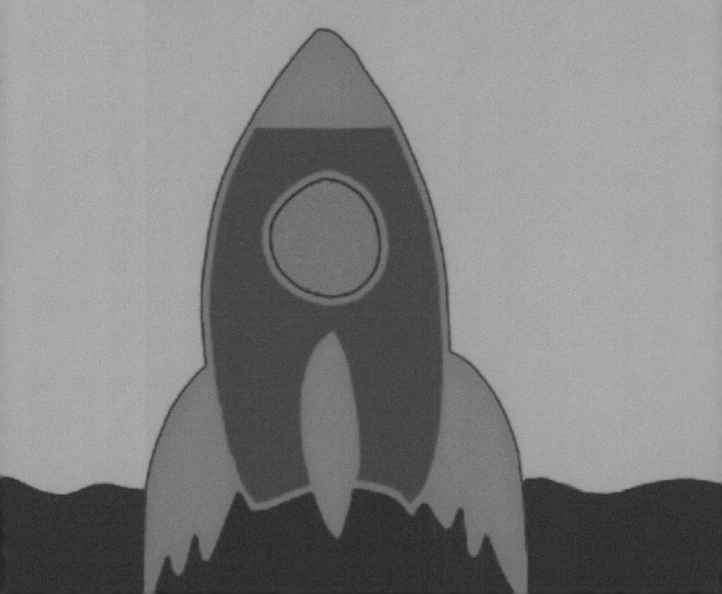

Getting so excited for this
adventure to begin,
beyond the stars to a
magical place.

Antonio got in his red rocket
and flew through the clouds.
Soon to arrive in outer space,
flying up for hours and hours.

Antonio arrived in the stars,
he admired the shining balls of light.
Earth looked tiny out his rocket ship's window,

it was such a beautiful sight.

Antonio turned
and saw the moon,
a big ball of
spotted grey.
It looked SO BIG
close up,
in space curiosity
leads the way!

Then there was the sun,
"WOW!"
Antonio thought.
Such a big ball of
FIRE,
seeing so much he
would go home and
report.

Antonio began to explore the planets
around our solar system,
he saw....

 Mercury,

 Venus,

Mars,

and Jupiter,

they all looked so amazing to him!

Then Antonio saw Saturn,
with its big and bright rings.
There are seven of them,
so much light each ring brings.

Antonio kept exploring space
and found the Milky Way.
It was lightyears in distance
with billions of stars,
so beautiful to look at all day.

It was time to travel home,
to Earth, to the ground.
Antonio had so much fun in outer space,
then he flew back home safe and sound.

At home Antonio arrived,
he stepped out of his rocket ship,
greeted by the ones he loves,
so excited to tell them about his trip!

Lightning Source UK Ltd.
Milton Keynes UK
UKHW050237060721
386527UK00002BA/109